Dear Parents and Educators,

Welcome to Penguin Young Readers! As parents and educators, you know that each child develops at his or her own pace—in terms of speech, critical thinking, and, of course, reading. Penguin Young Readers recognizes this fact. As a result, each Penguin Young Readers book is assigned a traditional easy-to-read level (1–4) as well as a Guided Reading Level (A–P). Both of these systems will help you choose the right book for your child. Please refer to the back of each book for specific leveling information. Penguin Young Readers features esteemed authors and illustrators, stories about favorite characters, fascinating nonfiction, and more!

The Bookstore Ghost

LEVEL 2

GUIDED READING LEVEL **I**

This book is perfect for a **Progressing Reader** who:
- can figure out unknown words by using picture and context clues;
- can recognize beginning, middle, and ending sounds;
- can make and confirm predictions about what will happen in the text; and
- can distinguish between fiction and nonfiction.

Here are some **activities** you can do during and after reading this book:
- Picture Clues: Reread this book and point to the pictures that help you discover who the bookstore ghost really is.
- Compare/Contrast: In the beginning of the book, Mr. Brown wants to get rid of the mice in his bookstore. He thinks they are scaring his customers away. By the end of the book, Mr. Brown feels differently about the mice. How do Mr. Brown's feelings toward the mice change from the beginning to the end of the book? Why?

Remember, sharing the love of reading with a child is the best gift you can give!

—Bonnie Bader, EdM
 Penguin Young Readers program

D0047086

*Penguin Young Readers are leveled by independent reviewers applying the standards developed by Irene Fountas and Gay Su Pinnell in *Matching Books to Readers: Using Leveled Books in Guided Reading*, Heinemann, 1999.

For Nick—BM

For Becky—NW

Penguin Young Readers
Published by the Penguin Group
Penguin Group (USA) Inc., 375 Hudson Street, New York, New York 10014, USA
Penguin Group (Canada), 90 Eglinton Avenue East, Suite 700, Toronto, Ontario M4P 2Y3, Canada
(a division of Pearson Penguin Canada Inc.)
Penguin Books Ltd., 80 Strand, London WC2R 0RL, England
Penguin Group Ireland, 25 St. Stephen's Green, Dublin 2, Ireland (a division of Penguin Books Ltd.)
Penguin Group (Australia), 250 Camberwell Road, Camberwell, Victoria 3124, Australia
(a division of Pearson Australia Group Pty. Ltd.)
Penguin Books India Pvt. Ltd., 11 Community Centre, Panchsheel Park, New Delhi—110 017, India
Penguin Group (NZ), 67 Apollo Drive, Rosedale, Auckland 0632, New Zealand
(a division of Pearson New Zealand Ltd.)
Penguin Books (South Africa) (Pty.) Ltd., 24 Sturdee Avenue,
Rosebank, Johannesburg 2196, South Africa

Penguin Books Ltd., Registered Offices: 80 Strand, London WC2R 0RL, England

Text copyright © 1998 by Barbara Maitland. Illustrations copyright © 1998 by Nadine Bernard Westcott.
All rights reserved. First published in 1998 by Puffin Books and Dutton Children's Books, imprints of
Penguin Group (USA) Inc. Published in 2012 by Penguin Young Readers, an imprint of Penguin Group
(USA) Inc., 345 Hudson Street, New York, New York 10014. Manufactured in China.

The Library of Congress has cataloged the Dutton edition
under the following Control Number: 98013809

ISBN 978-0-14-130084-9   10 9 8 7 6 5 4

THE BOOKSTORE GHOST

by Barbara Maitland
pictures by Nadine Bernard Westcott

Penguin Young Readers
An Imprint of Penguin Group (USA) Inc.

Chapter One

Mr. Brown liked three things:

ghost books, cheese, and cats.

"I will buy a bookstore,"

said Mr. Brown.

And he did!

He sold only ghost books.

Then he said, "I need a friend.

I will get a cat."

And he did!

His cat did not like fish.

But she loved cheese.

Mr. Brown and his cat ate cheese

for breakfast, lunch, and dinner.

They lived above the bookstore.

Mice lived in their house, too.

Chapter Two

One day, a woman came

in to buy a book.

She saw a mouse.

"Eeeek!" she screamed.

She ran out of the store.

A man ran out, too.

"The Black Cat Bookstore

has mice," they said.

Nobody wanted to come to the store.

"This is your job," Mr. Brown

told his cat.

"You are the cat.

You catch the mice."

So the cat went to the mouse hole.

The mice were scared.

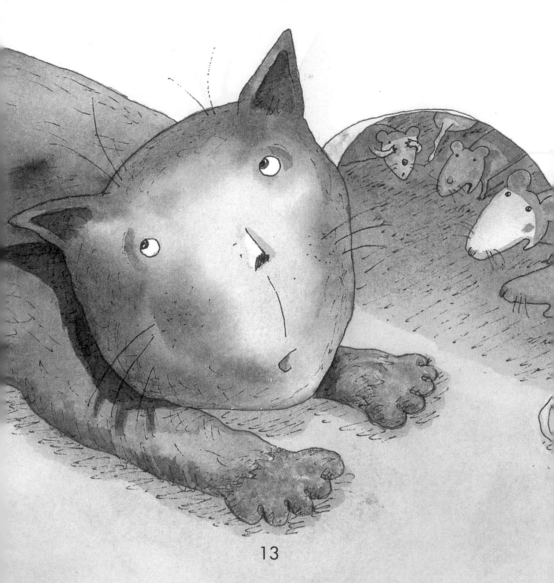

But the cat said,

"I am not like other cats.

I like mice."

And she did!

The cat and the mice played

together.

Mr. Brown was not happy.

"Those mice are scaring people

away!" he said.

"If they do not come in to buy my books, I will have to close the store down.

You have three days to catch the mice," he told his cat. "Tomorrow is day one."

"Mr. Brown says you are scaring the people away," the cat said to the mice.

"But this is a *ghost* bookstore," said a mouse.

"It *should* be scary."

Then the cat said, "I have a plan."

Chapter Three

Day one came.

Day one for the cat and day one
of the plan.

A boy was walking by the store.

CRASH!

A book fell off a shelf.

THUMP!

Another book fell on the floor.

"Did you see that?" said the boy.

He went into the store.

CRASH! THUMP!

More books fell.

"The Black Cat Bookstore

has a real ghost," the boy said.

Then his friends came into

the store.

Day two came.

Day two for the cat

and day two of the plan.

The store was very busy.

People came to see the ghost.

The cat purred.

Her plan was working.

PURRR...

On day three, the store was
busier than ever.
At the end of the day,
there was only one book left!
"I will not have to close the store
down after all," said Mr. Brown.
"Tonight, we will celebrate.
We'll have a cheese feast."

Chapter Four

"I like my ghost," said Mr. Brown.

"But I still don't like those mice.

Have you caught them?"

The cat purred.

She rubbed against

Mr. Brown's legs.

Then she walked away.

"Shall I follow you?" he asked.

He followed her to a bookshelf.

"Maybe I will see my ghost,"

he said.

The mice waited for him.

They pushed the last book off

the shelf.

CRASH!

The mice looked at Mr. Brown.

Mr. Brown looked at the mice.

"I see," said Mr. Brown.

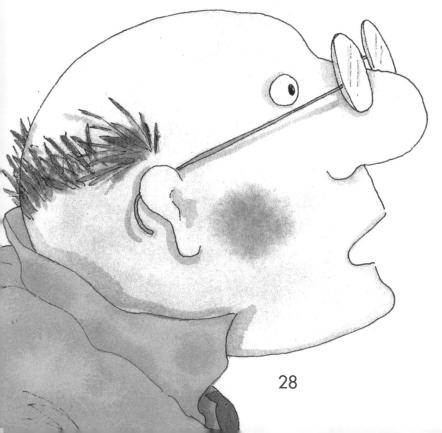

"Do ghosts like cheese?"

he asked the mice.

Now they all live together.

The store is always busy.

And Mr. Brown likes four things:

ghost books, cheese, his cat . . .

and his ghost!